Original
Published by Free Mu

SKIMPY

Ralph Borghart * Wilda Stek *
Marjo Swart * Stephan Schalkwijk *
Sjoerd Vrakking

America Star Books
Frederick, Maryland

Credits
Illustrations and cover design: Sjarrel Vrakking
Photography: Wilda Stek and Ralph Borghart

Softcover 9781633825161
PUBLISHED BY AMERICA STAR BOOKS, LLLP
www.americastarbooks.com
Frederick, Maryland

1.

TILE

"If you're lucky, you know that it is not a requirement to have it."

A tile with this wisdom used to hang in my grandmother's hall. I asked her how she had come there but old age or dementia made sure that she had to stay. She owed me the answer. Before I could ask if she knew what it meant to her, she said: *"I do not know what it means but it sounds good right?"*

I nodded but secretly I thought it was a high tile with content from Paulo Coelho.

After reading The Alchemist, I had the feeling that I had to read a nice, entertaining tale. I certainly do not think that my life is now immensely enriched unlike a few friends of mine.

One of Coelho's books had been given to me as a gift from my girlfriend and *Love* and *Life* which was given by my mother which excels to me but not in depth.

Sayings like *"Love is able to change someone and here, I discovered who I was,"* or *"The cup of suffering is not the same size for everyone"* for me as a package scrap with a thin layer of chromium (quite the philosopher and artist Henk Westbroek): it looks nice and seems a lot but it's nothing.

The pinnacle however was what I was facing in my student days. The book *The Celestine Prophecy* by James Redfield would be a *"spiritual adventure"* and a *"search for the truth."* There was also a matching workbook that would change your life and there were workshops. Your world would never be the same after reading the book.

The latter was true.

The Celestine Prophecy was a turning point in my life. All the books I've read after were much better, more exciting and profound and that includes the complete works of *Kluun*.

The scope of the Celestine Prophecy was that everything is energy and that energy vibrates.

Well I know more things that need power to vibrate but there is no need for me for all the books to be transferred.

Pomposity

Empty words

Vast Emptiness

Whipped air

I think I'll make a tile of late: "*Only those who do not believe that it exists will be able to experience true emptiness.*"

Eat that, Paulo Coelho!

2.

SORRY

What is a beautiful life together? You can even go with your body in such raunchy, filthy places or parts thereof and stop into things and your soul remains untouched and pure. You put your finger, nose or other body part with an excellent little boy or girl, which of course is not allowed but when you just feel like it sometimes, you just confess and wham, all is forgiven for you.

Even U.S. presidents and top athletes know this wonderful principle. They are enjoying the fuck out of wedlock. They are guilty of abuse of power, corruption, discrimination, scams, things that are not legally allowed but give them such a nice feeling. Of course they hope that it remains a secret but when it is discovered, they just say "*sorry*" to the world, let a few tears roll and ***all is forgotten again.***

Whether you throw yourself full of alcohol and smell like it doesn't matter; after all it is your day, your life. You forget the world around you and smash it good to go. You tram cubicles, shop windows, keepers, agents, passers-by and nothing makes you whole. Let yourself go, throw it out. Now enjoy it to the fullest because you don't know anything more about tomorrow. If there are witnesses or images are made, you'll just say '*sorry*' and your punishment will be mild. Just sorry and you can get on with your life with a clean soul.

What good do you really want to do? Just say sorry and all is forgiven and forgotten.

I therefore proclaim *sorry* as the word of the century. I know of no other word that is both used more meaningfully and meaninglessly than sorry.

This is a tribute to *sorry*.

3.

"THE ONLY PLACE WHERE HAPPINESS IS EXERCISED IS IN THE DICTIONARY"

It is an autumnal twilight. Dry beech leaves had been thrown through the autumn storm against the window. Condensation is dripping from the windows and the gas rushes. It's almost dinner time and the room of the Christian Daily employee's calendar fills with the smell of bratwurst and carrots when his mother arrives.

"Put it away Bernhard," she says. *"You've done enough today, let's eat."*

Bernhard tilted the transparent plastic with the Persian cloth, flannel, submitted writings and dictionary in *tafella*. His mother grabs a white linen dress with embroidered flowers and puts it on the plastic. Then the signs came.

Four layers, thought Bernhard. Can I grab that protective layer? Even with four coats, a snowman must still be cold. There's nothing in it. No lesson and no moral boost for the reader. Just think, even with four coats, a miser has no warm heart. No, that's all nothing.

There is no hit today. It's already November and he has yet to make ten spells for the edition of 1961. The calendar has four permanent staff. He must provide 90 spells per year. Every Sunday, he puts himself on the living room table with a notebook and a dictionary. The encyclopedia is standing behind him in the closet. The radio softly plays Hilversum 1.

While Bernhard is the worst at showing his good taste, his mother was chatting over the news in the neighborhood, engagements, births and illnesses. Bernhard realizes that he is satisfied with his wrinkle-free existence. No stress or exertion.

6

If you do not set high standards, you'll have a quiet life. Ecstasy and passion are dangerous. He does not like the pounding of his heart, sweating or flushing.

Somewhere on that windy night, the desert long behind them, Bernhard is saying about happiness, effort and the dictionary itself in the womb.

You do not take spells seriously, just as horoscopes, natural remedies or religions. They are all made by Bernhard with a stomach full of sausage and chocolate custard.

4.

PARSVOTTANASANA

Happinez is a glossy magazine with the subtitle *'mind style'*. I browse through it and see advertisements of luxury cosmetics brands, exotic destinations from Compeed and the **plaster** that protects you from the discomfort of your expensive towering heels. You can train to be a transformational coach or synthetic counselor of the psyche. You'll learn yoga exercise called *Parsvottanasana*. It's a lateral bending forward then you say, *"The light in me greets the light in you."*

There are many buying tips: traditional Swedish clog that you buy for 25 euros at the garden center but a trendy version costs 169 euros, sambal collection *"to cherish,"* and cheese made according to the Caring Dairy principle. There are editorials about Kabbalah, Veggie Day on Thursday or have the island feel of...no, not Ameland but Clare Island, an Irish island that *"requires a serious consideration"* to which the text is added: *"Take your herbs suitcase!"*

In the heart of it is a true family game: *The Snails*. The prerequisite is to first have a search for the garden snails as a pawn! In short, *"happiness"* is compressed into a glossy paper of about 150 pages.

I see this is all for me and I am the target. You can lose yourself in spirituality. There were women on the grand balcony, their penthouse overlooking the historic downtown or sitting and lying on their lounge sofa in their farmhouse whose stable has been converted to a salon. The barn doors have been replaced by an imposing facade of glass.

Is that happiness? Having the money that allows you to set things and where nothing is missing in your life?

There is also another form of happiness. That Willem for example who calls himself "*Livingstone*" is the eccentric from the Showroom program Joris Linssen. He has a well-cut tongue with the character of a Siberian husky (he says) and had been around for 40 years in a wooden hut between the animals in a forest. He wants nothing more. There's also snowboarding Bibian from the program *The Reunion*. She is a six-time Dutch champion. Her leg had to be amputated due to bone cancer. Just seven months after the amputation, she became champion again.

"Yes, you should do it with them. I make something beautiful."

The probability of metastasis is still there. She gives life a night.

Of course, there are no everyday examples but also to the ordinary m/v, it's a lucky game. As you can see, a friend of my eldest son for example recently sent a card within a bunch of flowers and it's addressed to "*my dear parents*" and she had never called her friend's parents before!

Well, this is not to be found in a magazine or TV program but there's a small fortune in the flower vase from a daughter with *Happinez* underneath it as the placemat.

5.

IN YOUR DREAMS

We drove a distant cousin through traffic in a borrowed car. Hank was my driver. I must confess that this is not entirely to my satisfaction. Hank was quite aggressive as he sat behind the wheel.

My father was suddenly taken in critical condition in the hospital and we feared for his life. Hank was standing next to me when I received the telephone call. He, Hank and no one else could help me and I just had to take this option because there's no other initiative. At first I was too stunned to act and I sheepishly showed myself on the seat post. I was already sorry less than half a minute later. On the German curses I noticed that my friend was very tense as he said some German curses. His *'German'* scolding was Hank's response to stress.

Crying was accompanied by the horn and obscene gestures of the middle finger. The speed limit has been exceeded by far. He would make a departure from the normal way every now and then. We were almost stuck in a green belt with spinning wheels and splashing mud. Mothers with prams were stewing terror as they moved apart. If a *'hero'* is once unleashed, nothing will keep him more in check. It was incomprehensible but we reached the hospital without any damage. The car was parked in front of the brutal ambulance. Then we ran to the information desk. Without any hesitation, Hank passed the queue and pushed the woman who was being helped at that time on the side. When she indignantly responded, Hank made a threatening gesture with his fist. With his 130 kg and 1 meter and 95 build, that made a big impression.

Everything soon meant a little when we searched for the Intensive Care! It is about life and death. The desk assistant winced and replied with a squeaky voice. We quickly ran to the elevator and found the ICU on the fourth floor. A too thick sister in a too short skirt caught us.

Unfortunately, we were too late. The patient was deceased. The family had already said goodbye. We could still see the patient. She went for us and showed us into a dim room and turned and reminded us to be calm. She spoke the words: "*Let your dreams and happiness come to you.*"

Okay?

My father lay in the hospital bed, unrecognizable. This is what disease does to a person.

Crying, I went on my knees and kissed his crossed hands. Hank was with beaten down eyes in a corner. Emotionally, I remained sitting like that for some time.

The ringtone cut through my sobbing. It was dearest sister. What have I done? Everything happened so fast with my father. My father was what? But…what? Which hospital?

My heaven, we were in the wrong hospital with the wrong corpse.

Look, after such a story, I think you should start at the abolition of that mortgage.

6.

HARDY

A frozen ground is hard to dig in especially with a regular shovel. It was therefore important to work ahead before the groove seriously freezes over. Henk made a series of pits *'in advance'*. On All Souls' Day, he made an estimate. He counted the octogenarians, the terminally ill and charged an extra for a drowned child or fatal birth. Usually he was right. In the spring, he usually had a hole about.

Henk was our neighbor. In the winter he wove baskets, sits on the ground with a plank between his knees. He never had the stove. His kitchen had this oil stove for cooking. If it was really cold, Henk would be with us in the kitchen, drinking coffee or eating soup. He liked to talk and expounded about the pastor, the church, the tombs or the sermon of the week. He went well and took the time to sit down. We listened with half an ear while we were busy with a mega puzzle of over 1000 pieces of Saint Bernadette of Lourdes.

It must have been the middle of winter in the fifties when Henk told us about the removal of his father's grave. The heater was on and there was a heavy smell of coffee, cigarettes and drying laundry.

"Yes, I was working on the grave of my father," sniffed Henk.

His nose was running and he did not have a handkerchief.

*"I thought, what will be left? The one time it was cheese, other times it's pretty dry and clear. You do not know in advance. Well, father neatly perished; **bone work** clean, neat skull and it was beautiful. His hair was still there. I recognized him right away: black hair, smooth back and without separation in the middle. Cool! I gently laid his bones together with the skull on*

top and just over the ironed hair. Normally all the bones go together in a large pit but for father I have done it in a box with a string around it. It was a nice reunion."

I suddenly thought of Henk 50 years later when I was planting bulbs with a spade in the garden. The ground was hard to hit by the tree roots. I almost could not get through. A spade deep, I saw something white shine about a spade deep. Bones! They were the thin bones of the mole that I had buried in the spring there. It was a dark creature with pink velvet gripping hands that had changed in the course of the summer into a clean and dry skeleton. I have the tulip loosely on top of them and closed the gap. No burial, no box and no string for this mole.

Cemeteries are now cleared with big brutal machines. The crossbones are violently shaken out of the ground. Henk has long been in his grave but even if he still has all his hair, I do not think there will ever be someone to gently iron over it.

SV

7.

PILLS

It's December and there they are again: the insurance companies with their **package comparison** and care advice and the self-styled independent organizations and Consumers Independet.nl with their call: *"Close your health insurance through us, you will get a group discount."*

Yes, just as much off as you get through your employer, union, or patient couch. You have to do your very best to get a discount off and if you want to have a specific question for a specific answer, you get the standard text of the general conditions.

"I can also find that *** yourself!" I yell at the e-mails of customers or consultants. Sunil Chris was the friendliest and answered my questions. What do these *'independent'* brokers make? All of them are scammers.

The municipal taxes go up. Why? My house has been devalued yet less than what I pay for property tax. I must be crazy. That's right; you pay less but waste more levy property tax at increased costs!

Hey there! The gardens will be maintained only once every two weeks for this year and last year, it had been every week! How much austerity is that?

Do I have to have an ad at the Nationale Nederlanden, one that's decorated with strawberries and whipped cream pie? After which, a cheerful question follows: *"Is your annuity free? Choose more security with more benefits and more fun."*

Yes, that is free, though, next year!

It was once an investment from the humble, hard-earned legacy of my good father. The insurers are what remain after the euro crisis which is still on, ladies and gentlemen. You are all there to become rich!

I read at the entrance of a doctor of general practice *"Dr. Pills on holiday from 24 November to 9 December"*. Inventing a name for a doctor would be a very bad joke but that was her real name!

"On vacation?" I wonder.

My own doctor is on the other side of town though and it seems that the GPs in this period are massive due to the holiday.

"Not surprising really," says the eldest son, *"with all those nagging people."*

Is that it? Are they trying to escape? Their patients are complaining precisely at a time when the patients are at peak. They will just often send in some youthful alternates with them who in turn send the patients away with a few *oxazepams*: those anti-stress and sleeping pills.

My younger son puts his hand on my shoulder and says with a wink: *"Ask yourself whether next year is more important."*

This is an aphorism of the young adult man helping his grumpy old man from his menacing blues.

＆．

○

How do you come up an iPhone, an iPad or an iPod or anything else with an *'I'*?

I have enormous respect for people who are creative and are successful with it too. I personally have not been successful. I'm pretty creative but cannot live. I'm pretty successful with my work but then again you have to pass a few creative endeavors. You cannot have everything.

You can be a billionaire and be adored by millions of nerds across the world and yet you are dead on your 56th year due to a rare form of pancreatic cancer.

Steve Jobs said it himself: *"Death is very likely the single best invention of Life."*

Death need to be creative, to think and create.

It's beautiful.

After a visit to India in the 70s, a young Steve Jobs came back as an ardent Buddhist. Steve also believed in reincarnation, he probably will return to earth again.

If ICEL.

7.
SUPERMARKETS

Today I'm going to cook Thai for friends. Delicious, I'm excited.

I've made a list of the supplies and some other things. I grabbed a plastic bag and walk to the supermarket. I want to grab a cart but do not have a euro. I go to the information desk with the employee behind the counter. Aunt Hilda's in good condition whether I do or do not allow them apparently, she does not give a fuck.

"Excuse me, can I have a change?"

By God's grace and with a deep sigh, I get my euros.

I'm looking for my necessary ingredients. In the produce department, I pick up onions and search for the *bok choy.* The latter is not at the place where it usually is. I'm looking for an employee to ask but that's not so obvious. I do not see anyone near the produce department. Near the chips section, I see a boy. He walks left.

"Can I ask you something?" I call after him.

He does not hear me and disappears behind the scenes. I see no one else in the store so I wait. He will still have to come back again. I feel that it takes at least 5 minutes before opening the double doors. I ask where I can find the *bok choy.* The employee looks at me with glassy eyes and says he will just ask and disappear through the swinging door. A moment later, he comes back with a colleague who didn't have a very intelligent look in his eyes.

"You had a question?"

"Yeah, I'm looking for bok choy."

"What? Pakzooi? What does that look like?"

Oh, my God...I walk him to where the *bok choy* should have been. It is now an empty shelf. Unfortunately, the ticket at the counter could prove that this is supposed to be there and now they lack the *bok choy*. The boy has no idea but was still looking back at me. My patience is almost taking off. Meanwhile, I continue to collect my products: rice, shrimp and cilantro. Where's the coriander?

The boy had come back and said they have no *bok choy*.

"How about coriander, do you have them?" I asked.

Sighing, he turns around again to disappear through the swinging doors. I start to get annoyed and try to finish what's on my list. How about toilet paper? It cannot be that the typhoid store had also forgotten to fill a stock of toilet paper. The boy in the aisle of the toilet paper section would prefer not to be here because I start to yell at him: *"It is not normal in this fucking store! It is not even complete with the toilet paper, only that sandpaper! Well, not for me!"*

Everyone really starts to walk my way. Sure Madam, go for it. I also understand that if you are elderly, you do your shopping on a Saturday afternoon because you have no time all throughout the week.

I drift further towards the coconut milk. In which aisle did they have that clogged again and where can I find the coconut milk?

"Beside the mustard, lady," stammers the boy who probably looks like Brian Wesley and can do nothing.

"Beside the mustard? Do you really think that I know where the mustard is? That stuff stays good for six years so that I do not have to buy it often, dick!"

The boy comes back and tells me that they have no coriander and as well as the cilantro. I'm sprawled on the ground as I stomped and screamed the whole lot together! I'm all done with this store! I put my cart away. I grab my euros which I obtained with difficulty to go out and leave the store.

With these thoughts, I tell my friends on the phone and they don't mind if there's no Thai food. Gosh, what a shame, I was just so excited!

10.

PONDWEED

Some years ago we bought our family an old house which was beautifully situated on a canal. The price was high. The money for the contractor was no longer there. We had to rebuild it by hand. Since we have been working on it for over a year, I must say it's an extremely stressful year. Afterwards, the same amount that was necessary for the contractor went to a marital and family therapist, we had previously could not have imagined. Everything worked out.

We live, as I said, next to a channel. This waterway was splitting our village in two. We run over the bridge daily from one side to the other. Such a bridge was convenient but it must not be opened and they do it! This is shit; it's irritating! Sometimes I stand for the barrier which four or five times a day off my precious time. I have a hernia. I ruined my marriage and hocked my last money to stand daily with my neck for a raised bridge with palpitations and red spots. If you see where the bridge opens, you have to blast your way through from annoyance! Inconsiderable *with* deeply-tanned manatees on the deck who, by excessive alcohol intake, were too apathetic to keep their eyes open. The old ones completely transform their retirement in marine diesel.

The machine devised for commercial and navigational watch system is completely paralyzed by this pondweed. This senseless recreation clogged our lakes and canals. What a waste of time for waiting. This *'wait sacrifices'* are in fact for each and every decent and hard-working citizen who was supposed to spend their money for these sailing wretches. A large part of these boat people are unproductive, they do not take part in the regular working life. This useless gruel adhered and concerned solely with the thwarting of the workforce.

What to do? I have considered moving but there's no chance with the current housing crisis. Another possibility is to drag a pair of barges to the bridge and drill a hole in the soil so that they will sink. This is at least, an impossible passage for some time.

Forget it; I'm not a hero. There is not much else to do but put a canoe in the canal and paddle with myself henceforth to the other side. As a pleasure boat passes, I ignored a pleasure boat as it passes.

That'll teach them the *lesson* with his head!

11.

A GRIM NIGHT

He knew it: behind that garbage were at least two people lurking. He picked up his golden staff a little bit firmer. The white satin of his glove stretched tightly around his old gnarled hands. Beside him, he heard the breathing of his faithful helpers. Although they had chopped often with this ax, it made him a strange kind of tension master to them. He wanted to do everything at least to avoid this to be their last journey through the outskirts of the city.

"Lokpiet, you lead them. Then sneak from behind Klauter Piet and Packet."

The Piet Signpost came from behind, a bicycle away.

"This is the only route that is still available, Santa Cluas. The roads that we used last year are all barricaded. Reconnaissance Piet via the roof would try to find an alternative route but I have not heard from them. "

The old man stroked his long white beard. A deep frown can be seen on his forehead. Previously this was only visible if he had somewhere to think this very carefully but he never left now.

"We'll do it the way I have just described, Petes. Lokpiet, you go first!"

"Yes, Santa Claus!"

Lokpiet came back from a car wreck and shuffled through the dark alley. Step by step, he walked hesitantly into the darkness until he completely disappeared.

"And now we wait, " whispered the old saint, barely audibly.

He could still remember the time when he and his helpers do not have to hide to deliver gifts but were met by hundreds of singing children who were waiting for them with flags and pennants. That was long ago.

About twenty years ago, the raids began. As he drove through the ghettos of the big cities on his faithful horse named *Amerigo*, he was increasingly attacked by groups of youths who are adamant and tossed gingerbread cookies or ice balls in his face while Amerigo kicked and beat as he makes his getaway. The lanky youth also threw fireworks in his direction causing severe burns.

Every year it gets worse until an annual pitched battle erupted on December fifth. In Rotterdam, there was a heavily armored bus and police escort from door to door to be driven in Utrecht in the morning. The ME in the afternoon had some quarters off and patrolled by army helicopters above the streets where he brought gifts around.

He was startled from his reverie by a noise from the alley. Someone threw something at them. It took the Saint some time before he saw what it was: the bloody hat of Lokpiet. When they came by the hundreds, there was a loud screaming of youngsters with caps, hoods and scarves just below their eyes. They waved stones and sticks and threw fireworks.

"This is the end," stammered the Signpost Piet.

The Saint sank to his knees and stared in disbelief at the deafening crowd that quickly came down on them.

"Comrades, cease your wild roar," he muttered yet.

Then everything went black. Only the moon was shining through the trees.

12.

ᏳLISSFUL

There we were, waiting in a long line of people to be blessed by Pope John Paul II. It was 1978. Years before, my parents felt they had to. In a good Catholic family, at least one of their sons should be called to the priesthood. I was the chosen one because I could sing in the church choir of my grandfather and because I was a loyal acolyte. I had once said that I found it so beautiful that the pastor was doing it behind the altar. As a 12-year old boy, they sent me to the Minor Seminary to follow priesthood yet knowing nothing about beatifications and having the knowledge about sexual abuse in the Church, there was nothing. I knew nothing at all.

It was a boarding school. We sleep in a 2x3-meter chamberette with only a bed, a wardrobe, a sink, a curtain as a door and a security guard at the venue. In short, a potential abuse contender.

My happiness and that of my fellow students was that it was a mixed religious community. There were also nuns who lived there. It was whispered among the senior students that the brothers did "*it*" with each other. What did "*it*" mean? We knew a lot of freshmen with whom the brothers and sisters lectured together with verve celibacy.

Sexual abuse of boys and sometimes girls by priests or even by nuns was the order of the day and we know now. Pope JP knew it too. There are, after all ecclesiastical condemnations of that time. These were not hung on the big bell. They did not know publicly how big the problem was and this pope is even beatified! Nota Bene Emeritus by Pope Benedict who also knew of the abuse!

Pope JP was beatified because he had cured a nun with Parkinson's. A second miracle is now eagerly sought that can give way to a canonization.

I know there is one. I call on Pope John Paul blessed yet on *"Heal the Dutch Cardinal Simonis's disease."*

He also knew about it and gave the famous words with the scandal: " ***Wir haben es nicht Gewußt.*** *(We do not know)* and added further: *"I find it terrible that those children were presented with their sex education that way."*

"Hold me!"

Idea: an escort for superheated clergy under the guidance of Mary Magdalene who whispered that she was once the courtesan of Christ.

Oh yeah…the meeting with Pope JP took place at Madame Tussaud's wax museum.

13.

MEETING

Exactly one year ago, a gentleman dressed in old-fashioned clothes stepped on me. His left eye peeked through a monocle and a gray goatee lined his sad mouth. With his bowler hat in his hand, he made a graceful bow. I could book a meeting with him: five euros for a four-minute meeting. Langer was also possible. The money went to India. I quickly figured out that this was twenty-five euros per minute. It seemed like a reasonable price so I paid a fiver and the meeting began. It was an extremely intense encounter where I don't want to forget every second.

It would change my life because from that moment on I have a new attitude to the phenomenon of "*meet*". Previously I never watched people, like so many others I met but what's there to lose? I was blind to the richness and beauty that lies in every encounter; disrespectful in a sense especially now that I've discovered how intense and subtle sensitivity can be met. But yes, you cannot blame an ignorant person. From that moment I wanted to immerse myself in everything that had to do with the '*encounter*'. Initially, I visited Mr._____ above once or twice a week but pretty soon it became more frequent.

The meetings were longer. Sometimes an encounter lasted 50 or 60 minutes. You understand it started to run properly in the paper and addiction performed. There was no time to work. I resigned and exchanged my clothes for salmon pink robes and let my beard grow. All my savings went to meetings. I wanted more and I started my international studies at the Academy of Encounters in Pune, India. To get money, I had my home and property on sale. I save money on the household through a water/bread diet and dropped thirty pounds. My wife and children have left. It did not touch me. It even strengthens me for the *'Greatest Meeter'* made me realize that there's no meeting without saying goodbye as there is no high tide without the ebbing of the tides.

My training in Poona was completed over four years. Only then did the study at being the Supreme Guru can begin. Again, long after the greatest magnitude glimmers comes a speed date with the blank, black NOTHIN...

SV

14.
OFF!

He was smaller than I expected but I recognized him almost immediately. His goatee was most striking. Of course, those unnaturally white teeth which sparkled even in the light of the lamppost.

As for the last question I took away with me was the fact that there are more than a hundred dogs who sat around him. He barely reacted when I got closer. He was full of ecstasy as he looked up at him, the alpha male, the top dog, the pack leader and the dog whisperer: *Cesar Milan!*

I felt that the line was no longer tight in my hand. *Choco*, my brown Labrador was sitting on his rump and was completely focused on Cesar. Like the other dogs, he gently began rocking back and forth while a soft but very melodic whine escaped from his throat. It sounded like Choco and the other dogs were singing, at least humming to it.

Cesar stood with his eyes closed between them, his hands in the air as if he conducted them. Suddenly he brought his hands down and did "*tsssss*" against the other dogs.

It was immediately quiet. A few hundred dog eyes looked at me and Choco threw me a reproachful look. Cesar opened his eyes and turned my way. He tilted his head slightly and turned his eyes to Choco who once briefly whined and lay down.

"*Your dog is unhappy,*" said Cesar. "*He's disappointed at you for being so late at night and that he gets a dog biscuit only once a week.*"

Choco barked twice. Cesar nodded and continued: "*On Sunday.*"

The sweat broke out from me. Why didn't I know that about Choco when he seemed so happy?

"But he's always wagging when I come home and then he jumps up on me!" I tried but Cesar shook his head.

"Choco does not see you as a leader but a weak and sickly creature that does not deserve to live with him in a house." Here Cesar showed a dramatic dropping of silence.

"I think it is better that you take leave of Choco and let him come to me."

With that, Cesar turned and put his hands in the air. The dogs began to sing again and rock back and forth. Choco also got up and got ready to go to them. I wanted to pet or hug him but I thought that this would be unappreciated by Cesar so I raised my hand as a last salute and whispered, *"Hello, Choco!"* but he was merged into the crowd.

I walked away in the direction of where I came from with the tail between my legs.

15.

MEET AND GREET

In two weeks, I will be leaving for the meeting of my life. Gosh, I'm excited for weeks and making preparations. My mustache will leave the Koran from front to back (and vice versa of course) and read, buy appropriate clothing, airfare, get a signed certificate of good conduct, confidentiality agreement, iris scan, fingerprints, DNA previously issued and what was even more necessary for the meeting with none other than Osama Bin Laden!

I joined the **bubble game** Allah lala on the Al Jazeera radio and won by singing a song. A meet and greet with good old Osama was paid in full with all the trimmings! Guess what? America should be at the back to interfere! They think they know the weather better. Everything's arranged in secret; naturally, no one was allowed to know where I was going.

But now I can open this up and honestly tell about my exciting adventure because it's over. Bin Laden is no more. Such a sweet man was all the while hiding in solitude. He also welcomed the meeting with me. We had already gone on Skype a few times and it was great fun; we laughed a lot. He looked forward to finally living back in the cave.

I would sing a song for him, the same song that I had won the prize for. I practiced it along every day but unfortunately, it cannot be. I'm a bit on the process but believe me, there is a very, very angry letter to Obama. I'll just do it and delicately explained to him how I feel about him and that is not tender. Obama, eat your heart out! An unarmed man can just shoot out of nowhere. No, make your horse, mister president! I'm not finished with you! A bit of my trip was thwarted! Luckily I get a consolation prize fro from Al Jazeera: a trip through Syria which is also exciting!

16.

DINNER GUEST

It is evening in Haverstraat. I take my bike lock and look a bit inwards with Marie who is already on the phone to make the dinner. I can see her sitting on the red velvet couch in her pink and bright green slippers. The curtains are only closed when she goes to bed. Everyone should see her there.

It was a special night. We ate hash: Marie, her friend Gertie and me. There was a bottle of mulled wine for the occasion placed on the central heating. Marie admitted she's a bit nervous because she had not cooked for years.

"You can eat three courses for seven euros in Overgooi hospital but I simply cannot bear to be alone. If no visit is over, I'm on the phone. The TV is on all day but that is not enough to dispel the loneliness. TV talks but do not listen and so it is. "

Marie grew up with 11 brothers and sisters and a resident uncle with loose hands. She married a boring man, who fortunately has been dead for 30 years so she can do what she wants now. She was 78 and tells beaming that sex is not over when you're old.

"No one can forbid you anything, right?"

She never had children, only a dog or cat because once again she has patience for that now. Every morning she gets up at seven and gets on the bike to the water spider to go swimming. She missed the huge swimming pool because it's been closed due to a bacterium. She pulls her sweater right up to show that she has a rash. It has been in the newspaper about the bacteria in the water spider and she is surprised that I am not as aware. There are scaly red spots on her skin under the huge flesh-colored bra that were dangerously and deeply constricted. *"I need to lose weight the doctor but I do not get down. You have so much when you're old!"*

While Gertie's coat in the hallway attracts cats to go to the home run, Marie whispers it quite strangely that Gertie want to have nothing to do with her children.

"They must have surely made it but that cannot be otherwise; glad that I do not have children!"

When I make preparations to go home, she tells me that they are just going to ask the neighbor if he feels like it tonight because it's still early. She puts drinks and a beer ready for him every Friday: *"He has a disabled woman in rehabilitation, so..."*

On the bike going home and slightly dazed with the mulled wine, I try to evaluate my acquaintance with Marie. It all started during the challenge. It was raining and blowing and many people stayed home. In the middle of the empty church square was a dreary stall followed by a numb but very genteel lady. In the context of *'new social initiatives'*, she had a club founded with the name: TABLE GUEST. You wrote you there and then you get *'matched'* as a guest or as a cook that you could choose from. Then you can eat together at someone's home to take and meet a lot of other people.

Marie was my match. She will come to me next week.

17.

PHOTO

While clearing out the attic, I became bogged down by my old photo album, a jaded and faded booklet. I hop, skip and jump my youth in only one folder from infancy to adolescence because there was rarely a photographer at home with us. My mother made snapshots without the exception of abominable quality. However, the photos remain of great value to me. They take me to the past without effort.

For example, the colored plate of about 5 x 8 cm showed three boys of about 12 years old. The boys are very brown, their hair turned blonde and they sit under the awning of a tent. One of the boys was smoking a pipe. The history behind this picture was bubbling slowly. It's 1968, a holiday in Spain. Two large families camp on a mega site. The boy with the pipe was a cousin. In those days smoking was normal at 12 and at 14, you take your first pot and with a little luck, you will generously be on heroin on your 16th. The second man in the picture is cousin Jos and then me; I am the youngest.

The first thought that comes to mind is: what has inspired my parents to have six nagging children in an overheated car through a thousand miles of roads (the Route du Soleil did not exist then) and move down south? Were the summers in the Netherlands already so bad? It is incomprehensible to be dying in a tent after such a journey.

The only explanation is that my father had survived at a concentration camp in World War II. He had since been so positive and optimistic that he had to make a trip to Spain while on the bike (I see that matter in a camp or an alternative to Prozac).

Back to the photo, the trio was to listen to a tape shown by a cousin, a handy guy whose humor has taped to the spool for six hours. It must be my first contact with the idea of a cabaret. Before that time, Uncle Wim's humor was about a joke he told at this birthday with a lot of facial expressions and gestures but this was different. Every sentence was a joke or had a double bottom. The world was ironic and viewed rather seriously. I could not get enough of it and it had played in my mind for a few days that we have spent during the holidays to the irritation of my mother. We had spent many days before the tape recorder, giggling and chuckling. The tape was, among others, a conference of Fons Janssen's 'The Laughing Church'. This show was by far the most funny. Fons took "the Church," which in those days was an institution at the heel. You could earn spot money and it was a revelation! If we were not on the device, we imitated almost all the texts of Janssen with funny voices.

Humor makes you invincible.

1⋆.

AN EGG IS PART OF IT

My freezer has been broken for a while and it's quite annoying. There's no fresh bread or fresh vegetables for the taking or, if it suits me, a fresh egg! Fresh eggs from the frozen pizzas and chocolate ice cream is such a wonderful and fresh *option* on Sunday morning, cooked with bacon.

Yes, ladies, that, you had better have lying around in your freezer if you're 35+ and you want to confess the prince on the white horse of nowhere and you have rattling ovaries. If you then encounter the father of your children about five years, do you have fresh eggs? Single women, who are likely to be too old to have children, can have their eggs frozen for later use, even if there are no strict medical reasons.

Marieke Schellart had this vulnerable and personal dilemma portrayed in her documentary *"An Egg for Later"*. What do I really think about it actually? I would also like to make this choice. The emptiness that Marieke feels was filled by having a child. Is having children saving? It has to do with not being able to let go of that outlined ideal picture. Would I be on my 45th and still really want to be a mom? Or is it a reflection of our pampered Western culture, where we have to decide because we like to have everything in our hands?

Then I see Marieke who had injected herself for fifteen days for the use of retrieving the eggs. She was pricked out through her vagina with a thick needle with hormone injections in her stomach. They could have removed a piece of her ovaries with surgery and this freeze. Ugh.

Her frozen eggs still do it after thawing! Would that also be possible that we will freeze alive the egg, fish, or chicken? Thus we will have the solution for overfishing immediately! If we now freeze the fish alive, it can just swim back soon after thawing. Back with all the tuna and cod, they can hop, swim and make children so that we can catch an unlimited number of them again.

Let's go back to Marieke. She apparently thought about it and thought that this is what she wants now. If Marieke nevertheless did not use it to become pregnant, she can still have marinated egg sticks or fried eggs with garlic which of course are delicious!

17.

FAMILY

Recently, I was sitting with my wife in a restaurant. It was not crowded and not quiet but just cozy. Suddenly the atmosphere was disturbed by a noise in the hall as a young family entered: a father, mother, a boy and a girl. The kids had a conflict and fought it out loud. The trendily-dressed parents ran as if it did not concern them. The group sat down at an empty table. Mom and Dad looked at each with a neutral face in another direction as if they wanted to avoid each other's gaze. The children quarreled greatly. The talks stalled at the other tables. The ambiance was gone. Annoyance can be read on the faces of the guests. After some time, a young waiter volunteered at the club. Menu cards were distributed. The mother, who had hitherto spoken a word, began to converse in an overly flirtatious tone with the waiter. She laughed and it echoed through the room. The waiter was clearly uncomfortable under these conditions. After some scribbling on a notepad, he rose on his feet. The generous laugh that the woman had on her face froze in slow motion. The couple fell back into audible silence! The children ran screaming and banging around.

After five minutes, a *new* waiter arrived with a tray with two glasses of cola, wine and beer. Again, the woman began to *be* challenging, much to the anger of her husband with the waiter. This small success expanded. She *moved* her body and threw her blonde locks high again with a huge toothpaste smile.

"Now that's enough," cried her husband as he jumped. *"Go home!"* Mountains of pent-up anger came loose but the woman was slightly bruised. In a reflex, she picked up the wine and threw it in the face of the man who turned and strode on

high legs out of the restaurant. Delicious! Finally, the children fell silent. Dad had a flabbergasted face and a dripping head. After some time, he noticed the prying eyes of the audience so he grabbed his wallet and threw 20 euros on the table and bashfully shuffled the children after him, "*dripping*" off. A sigh of relief went through the crowd. The family: the cornerstone of society!

20.

CONVERSATION

Yesterday I saw a work of three infants hanging on the bulletin board next to the coffee machine. What were they doing there? At that time, I had no time to think about it but at home that night, I walked in once in the office with that in mind. In each room, I saw frames with smiling blue-band babies with mom and dad in the garden, on the boat or on the hockey field. They were sunlit idylls of civil happiness. At that time, the bell rang. It was Thekla, a matron of the allotment association with an excuse to come in for coffee. Before she could tell how a Pakistani lover cheated her and had overpowered me for the hundredth time, I took the initiative and asked if she ever had noticed that cozy family photos in the office? Eagerness is a soft expression of what can be read on her face. She took a deep breath and started talking: "*Yeah, well that's really stupid; we did not do that earlier. They're monkeys together after all. They do not want to do for each other, like, look at me with my family; you see how well I burped? That's all mine! I am a father, a cornerstone. All vanity with modern penis sheaths!*"

She sipped her coffee, put a heavily ringed hand on her bosom and went on: "*You have to remember how to put down any photos that look like your kids. It is pure harassment; it is offensive and discriminatory!*"

I raised my eyebrows and she went on: "*You do not count if you do not have a family, you do not exist if you have no husband, no children and no work! You are nothing, nobody. You do not meet the requirements! I never have to move to Bunnik .There's nothing for me to do there. They play with all the family there in their brick bunkers. They only come out to dive on the way to the grocery store with their giant people-*

carrier. I am bored to death in that God-forsaken Bunnik! No wonder I fell for the charms of Virsuninipad. He adored me; we would adopt three children with leprosy... "

She fell silent, stood up and turned around decisively on her block heels to tackle her coat. I let her out and was looking for a cheerful note: "*Hey Thekla, you know what our application manager has put on his desk? It was a picture of his hangover!*"

She looked at me with a look of contempt, makes a pirouette on her block heels again and stepped out the door. Through the window I saw a purple woolen cloak with a click-clacking walk to the bus stop...on the he way to Bunnik.

21.
WHAT SHOULD WE DO?

The attic should be cleaned up. The matter must stand against under all that old sheets but that does not seem to do: toys, old furniture, folders administration to full cabinets and cases without any logic and order. Behind some wardrobes, a **working angle** was created which has long ceased to be recognized as such. Even the self-built, hard-to-reach **item** is packed. Well, so it needs a cleanup.

The question *"what should we do?"* delivers heated arguments with family members, with all of that irritation. What will we bring to the waste station, to the Recycle bin, the Toy Fair and what will we put on the Marketplace? We keep what? The eldest son wants to preserve all the *Lego* and most of the furniture can go away. The youngest son wants his flute, which he once gotten as prize from the store. The spouse cannot waive meters of books even some of that misery falls apart and my vinyl collection then of the triple LP Box like the concert for Bangladesh by George Harrison for example? It's a collector's item. Check the internet to see what it produces. What? It's for 33 euros? I really need to get rid of it for that amount?

All those who just show up somewhere unexpectedly: the slippers of 45 years ago from the deceased father of the wife. She was ten years old and was kept as much as possible out of the disease from her father. You do that *"in the sunshine house,"* in between the dust as it was always called. She even had a birth announcement with the sounding name: *Leore*. That's what we have to do away with. We once made two versions, one for a girl and one for a boy. The girl was never built, it was the boy and then "The **Dagmissaal**" I got from a 12-year

priest student. It contains the texts to be read for each day of the year. During the mass on December 26, the anniversary of Saint Stephen, I read: *Beati Immaculati via, qui ambulant in empty Domini.* Happy are those who immaculately go through life and accomplish the law of God. Men, read that to your church leaders again! Do you understand what it says? Was it ritual burning or saving? We had a can of medals, including those of the Nijmegen Marches which I brought together with my son, when one of the youngest participants walked, shining with four months of training together.

Well, family life piled up in an attic. Is there still some way of clearing and cleaning it yet?

22.

DNA

In her neck was an armored bird's nest of thin white hair and black bobby pins. The white hair was the only bright spot in her appearance. She wore a calf-length coat of black wool crepe, georgette, monumental shoes and black stockings with a swinging seam all through summer and winter. Over the shoulders hung a dead fox, complete with head and feet. She was the archetypal grandmother from the 50s. Father had taught us to call her granny because we already knew a grandmother on mother's side. She took him and did not appreciate it and her look was grim with each greeting with granny.

She spoke in capitals and one of her regular expressions was: *"They've put the crown on your head."*

They thus referred to her five adult sons. My father, the youngest, heard it all and had long been suffering from it. Resistance was futile, that he knew as early as kindergarten.

Granny had diabetes. My parents saw with dismay how they feasted on fat bloater, cream and lemon gin under the lament: *"What God created, man enjoys."*

On a beautiful summer day, we were sent out to pick her up at the bus stop opposite the coal company. Mother baked a cake for Granny and father got a quick haircut. We were waiting along a dirt road between large mountains of anthracite. My mother had once again turned away much too early and I decided to go pick a bouquet of poppies for my grandma. All I thought about while picking was her grateful smile when I would hand it to her. My bouquet had elegant genuflection of Empress Sissi. My brothers decided to climb Coal Mountain. While they were on the top which I had come up for to scream, the bus arrived. Granny took her time to get out. I loved my bouquet and held it tightly and gave her my brightest smile. Granny's initially condescending gaze slid immediately to my brothers who slid on their ass from the Coal Mountain. In a flash, her face was familiar like storm and hail. She thundered: *"Where is your father? Who shall bring my suitcase? You are too dirty to tackle it. I'll carry my suitcase myself and you throw the weeds away and grab my umbrella. God help me what a reception! I feel like immediately want to return!"*

Granny and the boys set on a brisk pace. In the distance, I saw my mother standing by the front door. There was something in her attitude according to reports, in which I read that the cake had collapsed and my father did not come back from the hairdresser. In my hand a bouquet was stolen bald while a trail of red leaves was behind me.

I rattled off the tip of the umbrella along the fence of the neighbors and felt my face for the first time, folded to storm and hail.

23.

A WORD

I had time between appointments so I went to an unknown dime-a-dozen shopping to get a cup of coffee in an equally dime-a-dozen restaurant. I walked in, greeted the people behind the counter and saw a place on the bench against the wall. From here, I could easily see who else was there and who came. It was not very busy even though it was lunch time. I put my bag on the couch, took off my coat and put it over the back of my bag. I sat down. Next to me sat a young couple in their mid-20s that almost says, look what I did. They looked but when I nodded at them, they turned their heads. To give myself an attitude, I picked up the card. Not that I wanted to eat something, but still. The blonde waitress came and I ordered a cup of coffee, closely watched by the couple next to me. From my bag, I picked up the paper and opened it. I heard Jan Smit in the background.

The couple next to me had not said a word to each other.

On the other side of me was much too thick mother with her, it seemed, daughter. They both ate a bowl of pea soup. It smelled delicious. The mother could not eat further and asked if her daughter wanted to finish the food. The girl wanted it and feasted on the soup from her mother.

The couple next to me still had not said a word to each other.

I tried to read something in the newspaper looked at the picture of a smiling Lionel Messi with a golden ball in his hand but my thoughts were not with Messi, but the couple next to me. It fascinated me. How can it be that such a young couple has nothing to say to each other? I often see couples sitting in a restaurant where there are painful silences and I ask myself why they always go out to eat. Being together on the couch with the TV and your plate food is still fun. I had that image of the couple next to me.

There seemed to be some energy that comes from both of them and eyes twinkled a little when the waitress came with their sandwiches: a hot sandwich meat for him and a smoked salmon for her. They looked almost relieved at the sandwich and began to eat. She asked him a little later: *Nice?* He nodded, as he had his mouth full. Suddenly it was as touching as it was just as sweet. I sipped my coffee and smiled.

The couple next to me finally had said a word to each other.

24.

WHITE SILENCE

The Green Heart of Holland is covered with a thick layer of snow. At least 25 cm is already there on the towpath and drifting along the river ramparts. I plow through it, sometimes up to my knees. Hundreds of black birds, coots, were there on the snowy ice and their white beak extends into a fluffy shield like a big snowflake is on the forehead. Airborne, the flights of geese were in V-shape. I pass a dilapidated green wooden shed with the telltale Latin name *'Orare,'* or *'prayer'*. A drink stand for farm boys and girls would not look out of place. The land next to it was full of rubbish: barrels, crates, pallets, a trailer and a boat which, apparently, cannot be sailed. What is that all about? There is no access path; only the towpath which is sealed with transfer gates run past it which is a little further on the Ijssel Bridge. Before I get there, I have to squeeze myself between overhanging reeds. I have a beautiful view in the middle of the bridge over the adjacent marina and polders. Remanufactured barges, boats, camping rafts and boats are waiting on the oncoming spring. I see an abandoned caravan parked and the contours of the Ijssel stein against the background of a bright, even light-shimmering sky: the mill and the tower of the basilica, exactly in between a 375-meter high tower.

I decide to have a drink at the marina restaurant. It is empty. A small and round-shaped diner girl comes. She had funky shoes, long apron with images of anchors, ropes and flags, a flapping ponytail and bright red apple cheeks. A farmer's haven is exactly in this environment.

"One Jägermeister. "

"Coming!"

I sit staring out, enjoying the view as it was slowly getting dark. Half an hour later, the first restaurant guests arrived. He (where did you buy those?) was in burgundy pants, white jacket with the full width of the back "*Gaastra*". They also already have a balloon skirt underneath; I cannot see the shoes. Two children are named Caspar and Sophie T Jochie with a cocky Mc Gregor Hats on. The girl of course wears *Uggs*. They have a boat stuck here in the winter! My wet dirty trousers and walking shoes were in contrast with the rather tightly dressed family.

I step out once again and go back on the same path. I ignored the warning on the transfer gate: "*access only between sunrise and sunset*". There was light on the snow under the stars. The snow squeaks under my shoes. After half an hour, I stop for a moment and let it penetrate the area.

God, it's pretty quiet.

25.

ORANGE/GREEN

"They have cut all the roses away! That cannot be!" My roommate calls out.

All I noticed was that there was so much activity lately in the little garden of our house. Overalls were off and on. It started a few weeks ago when a Piaggio Pickup stopped for the square. A man got out, pulled a bright orange safety overall and put on a helmet and earmuffs and began to cut the lawn edges. Was that needed then? First, the grass should be mowed anyway but what's with the helmet and the earmuffs then? OSH is surely justified.

That same day at eleven-thirty, there was a guy on a bike. He inspected the playground equipment, crawled into a playhouse, kicked a seesaw and took notes. He seems happy. As he gets on his bike, there is a second man who did the same check again! Well, the church should not take any risk. The time I swam in watercourses, the irresponsible rickety tree houses built in local trees is far behind me.

A day later, another male grabs a broom from the container and brushes the sign that warns you not to leave dog shit and keep it clean.

A week later, a whole delegation of bright orange-clad guys were piercing dirt, weeding, pruning the rose bushes and were digging out. The little garden is very fresh just like spring. Why?

I'll ask one of the guys.

"Crisis, sir; the municipality has decided to cut back on green. Half of the trees are being felled and from the parks, the squares and green spaces, we get a quarter of shrubs and plants away. Next year, you will not see us."

"*Why?*" I ask.

"*The congregation joins Green. Do you have that?*"

"*What?*"

"*Well, that just a project for the weather. The residents have to take care of the cleaning and maintenance of their streets and the greens itself. You need to start placing leaf baskets. The neighborhood itself must rake the falling leaf together and put them in baskets. Half of us will be put on the streets; the other half should give people tips on maintenance, cooperation and lend materials and tools.*"

"*How do they organize the hell?*"

"*I do not know. In a few months, you'll get the Green Paper. They'll contain everything.*"

I am wholeheartedly in favor of making my own living environment. Citizens should share responsibility but if you do not properly organize the neighborhood, it's still a mess. Do you need to go green? How? If the animal police are now retrained to green police who will see that we cut in with safety overalls and helmet and earmuffs on the lawn edges?

SV

26.

WAKE UP

She slowly wakes up and turns around again nicely to be under her flowered comforter. She hears the birds chirping merrily outside and the sun is shining strongly through the curtains in her face. Nice and slow to wake up. She sees him and remembers the wonderful night they had. She crawls to her love and puts his arm around him. He moans, satisfied. She is still in bed for half an hour, stretches wide and stands up, pulling a red shirt and running down. She first put the coffee on, plain old filter coffee that she finds the best. She faces her CD rack and looks at all the CDs that she has collected over the years. She likes to buy more CDs with certain bands they have seen live. She chooses an album of Tom Waits, Blue Valentine, and later heard the heavy dark whiskey voice of Tom across the room. With a cup of black coffee without sugar in her hand, she hums along with Tom as she stands by the window. She stares thoughtlessly ahead. Suddenly she felt two hands on her and kissed her neck. Love is awake. He pours himself a cup of coffee and stands beside her. Together they stood silently by the window, both with a satisfied, happy smile.

He is sleeping with her again tonight under her terribly flowered quilt. He wakes at the loud chirping of birds and finds the sun shining on his face annoying. She was lying against him and irritated, he moans and turns slightly away from her but she in turn remained with him for another half hour. Fortunately, she stands up and he hopes that she'll start brewing coffee. He hears her down the stairs and goes lying in the bed. Delicious: alone in bed. He hears that she deliberately played Tom Waits…again? He does not think they have many CD-buying programs, downloading is much cheaper. He wants to have an espresso and gets up hungry. Downstairs, she stands by the window and he walks softly to her. He surprised her and kisses her neck. The stale air at the pub is still in her hair. He sees that there is no espresso but filtered coffee. He pours himself a cup of coffee, sits down next to her and silently stares into her garden with her. He realizes that he has not said much. Last night was fun, but he will be good to go home again after coffee. He hopes that she doesn't have a crisis because he has no sense.

27.

NARCISSISM SHOULD BE YOUR PLAN

When I'm in the family to tell us how the whole family in a dilapidated blue Opel drove to our cottage on the beach, everyone is excited about the beginning of my story. One says: *"All of us never went to the beach because mother never wanted it."*

The other: *"We had no beach house; we had to put on our bathing suit with a large towel around us. It was Aunt Hilda who had a beach cabin. Sometimes we were there by the grace of God to make use of it."* Another might add: *"The Opel was tatty but just used and besides, it was green."*

Then we try to get together around our memories:

"Father had a car but no driver's license."

"Jill threw a whole Tupperware drum with sandwiches in the sand."

"No, that was Guusje! We had just tapped out the sandy sandwiches and ate that up!"

"You've always been a dreamer!"

"Not at all, you do not know how the sand crunched between your teeth and how Gretel had hidden to escape the collective anger of the family for the rest of the day in the dunes and how they then ended up in the corner of the lifeguard, where father has taken her!" Then roaring: *"No it was not like that then and it was much later when mother had sewn 'a new bikini for Gretel from white terry..."*

Jill remembers absolutely nothing about it or maybe she's just pretending.

I look forward to catching up with childhood memories in the bosom of the family. You'll never get beyond your first sentence and before you know it, you're the target. I do not talk about the past with a young company. A long time ago, my children have images for the youth of the rigid historical black-and-white newsreels. Some imagination is needed to color these things. You also need to explain more and more. Who knows even the wringer, the suspender and who does still scrapple? Moreover, if you are not careful you are going to repeat yourself and you can see the youthful audience share pitying glances.

Too bad because to tell about the past is a giant ego trip: you can run rampant through talk and portray yourself as you please. Childhood is an immense source of pleasure, provided among peers and with strict avoidance of family.

2.8.

EARLIER

Long ago, in my early childhood, around 1960, indoor playing was not so in vogue. Most of the day, children were brought outside from the moment they could walk. It was in the days when the parish priest parishioners arranged an accretion. The principle that every ovulation should be firm with a dollop of semen finished and literally threw a fruit. The families were then so great that my family was among those in the middle with only six children.

Opposite us, for example was attended by the Raven family, they had ten girls. Mother, a grumpy fat chick with loose hands, spent little time raising her daughters. Conniving chicks formed a mob underway in our neighborhood. Slightly further afield was the Roekel family; they had 11 boys! Dad was a chimney sweep and a handyman and he did not take it so closely. His little things were never corrected; they were vicious fighters without exception better than where you could ride around. Fortunately, there were also fewer mean children in the street so I had no shortage of playmates. It was often so busy in our "*corner*" that you could not tell the difference between our street and a full school. Incidentally, the outside tarry was completely harmless, there was barely motorized traffic. The bicycle or a horse-drawn carriage was the means of transportation. In our street, exactly two cars were parked: a gray Volvo kattenrug and a green VW Beetle 1200. The latter was owned by an older couple that was only used when absolutely necessary and when it was not raining, the car started. The Volvo was a representative. He rode it every morning at eight o'clock with a breakneck speed through the streets. This was the danger that day ceased to six hours because the race with the same blood sample came back in the hallway.

As mentioned, the street was thick with children. All classes were represented. Play was a feast. There were a number of condemned homes in our village where you could make wonderful den of thieves. There are also some undeveloped fields ideal for hide and seek, fido stabbing or football. The school was without a moment of boredom as well as at home where play is always spent outside. The world was a paradise. House arrest was the toughest and meanest punishment that a child could get. We prefer to concede with fifty lashes.

Suddenly the phenomenon of *'playing outside'* changed. On Wednesday and Saturday afternoons, around one to four hours, it became an empty street. An observant person could link with the first television programs for children, "*the children's hour,*" Pipo de Clown and the streets went empty.

Then it started: television! There is nothing that can beat that!

27.

SHAVING

Like any little boy without a beard, I was fascinated by the ritual of my father's shaving. I stood next to him every morning at the sink with the shaving brush dipped in soap and shaving his face covered with painted white foam. Only this part of the shave, I found it all extremely fascinating.

What came next was even more spectacular. My father took his razor, (an heirloom, I believe) held it against his cheek and clipped a long way. For years, I believed in the fact that the sole purpose of shaving was to get shaving soap made just back from your face ASAP. The realization that there was a relationship between the facial hair of my father and the sharp edge of the razor came later.

I was six years old when we're two weeks in the Sauerland, like every year at Christmas. A red Audi 100 where we drove through the snowy mountain landscape was white and the road to the hut we stayed was a big sliding party. The suitcases in the rooms were slammed. My mother once made a cheese fondue that's a little too thick and which my father received with standard diarrhea as we fell after the compulsory round of *Generations* or *Parcheesi* into a deep, dreamless sleep.

The next morning I was the first to wake up on my toes (not to gently do, I always walked on my toes). I walked to the bathroom. I flipped on the light and saw my father's shaving razor on the sink. I took a few steps forward and grabbed the razor bite. I balanced it carefully in my left hand, picked it up in my right hand and put it back because what will you do with a razor if you do not even have the beginning of a mustache or beard? Exactly! I grabbed the knife, brought it to my right eye and shaved in a smooth motion of my right eyebrow off.

A few seconds later, I realized what I had done. What if the space above my right eye would forever remain hairless?

Then I remembered that I had long bangs and in the 70s, it was in fashion and could come very useful now. I raised my eyebrows (or whatever was left of it), so they just disappeared under the edge of my pony. Perfect! If I could keep it the whole week, the hairs will perhaps grow back.

At the breakfast table, I had a moment of illusion that I got through with something until I noticed that everyone was staring at me and my dad asked me why I looked so surprised all the time. I burst into tears so when I closed my eyes, my eyebrows were visible.

I received own shaving kit on my 13th birthday from my father. If I ever have kids, I'll keep those under lock and key.

30.

SCHEDULE

I played with Barbie with a friend. Usually we were models or actresses; that was always the world we wanted to go with all our glitz and glamour. This was probably because I knew this would never happen for me. I had thick glasses and fashion models and actresses don't have that unless I play the daughter of Freek de Jonge again though. I stole doll clothes from a friend, played in the haystack and crawled through the homemade perilous passages or went to get sweets at Aunt Sister. I also went dressing up. I played through a shop decorated with knickknacks to impose the sidewalk and wait for the hole where I once saw someone come out and whoever wanted to buy anything. We played mommies and daddies and baked cookies. I bullied other children but I was also bullied myself. I grew up as an ordinary child, according to schedule.

Little Moammar built sandcastles for hours or dug trenches and tunnels in the sand. He also baked cookies and shortbread. He often sat at the Bedouin tent and played with his friends whom he affectionately called *"rats"*. If he wanted to play with his friends, he'd go to their tent and cry: *"Come out of your caves, dirty rats!"*

"Your boyfriend Moammar's there," said the mother's boyfriend then!

They played soccer in the sand barefoot where Moammar's camps are divided: one camp against the other. Moammar had certain rules. He also played with guns, bombs and grenades just like any child of that age. They shot fighter jets from the air and Moammar became very angry when one of his friends conceived a *'no fly zone'*. If he was angry, he was always screaming and he repeated his phrases to convince the others.

His mother would smile and would always give him a cup of tea. They also played mommies and daddies and began to dress like one. As a child, he really liked to dress up and pull on those colorful robes that you know. Moammar also liked playing in the herb garden where he gained inspiration for his book later, among other things and it's called "Escape to Hell and other stories". He gives his views on various topics on this book including herbal medicine. Children who did not want to play with him preferred death or get taunted around until they cried and begged for mercy. It was reasonably balanced. Moammar Gaddafi also grew up as an ordinary child, according to schedule.

31.

OUTWITTED!

On an early spring day, we paddle on the canoe route calls to Leerdam on the Lustige Linge like the outdoor site ontrack. nl. The directions we get next were atmospheric drawings and idyllic pictures with what seemed to be nature education. We read: "Completely motionless, with his shoulders hunched and head down, the blue heron stands along the waterfront. He is very smart and his attitude was well thought. He does not budge and makes his neck longer. He remains rigid to look in a direction, arches his neck to a big "S" and disappears with his head and beak as a spear underwater. He comes over and outwitted his prey: a minnow.

Gone is the fish, dead.

The word "*death*" gets a very wry sense when I think of a number of recent events. One was a crashed bus with schoolchildren returning from a skiing holiday in Switzerland. It took 22 children and six counselors' life. Children who survived the crash said that the driver was exchanging a DVD. Presumably he did so many times before with "*two fingers in his nose.*" This time it was fatal.

"*Hi Mom, hiking and skiing was great,*" writes Marie-Lyne on her web diary.

"*Where were you goddamn it?*"

Then there's the civil war in Syria. Thousands of civilians are humiliated, tortured and shot down by the security forces of President Bashar al-Assad. Children with their throats cut are found while the Hitler of the Middle East is watching Harry Potter. "*Good woman*" Asma-a highly educated daughter of a British-Syrian cardiologist and her marriage invested a star and banker she shopped and comes home with expensive necklaces, a Ming vase Luce and a pair of Christian Louboutin pumps.

"World, what will we do about it?"

What a contrast: the violent death of innocent children in the prime of their lives and the "self-chosen death of world stars like for example Michael, Amy and Whitney! Surnames are not needed, everyone knows them. They could not afford the luxuries of life and lost to alcohol and drugs. The Dutch queen cover *Oosterhuis* made a tribute album after the death of Michael. She selflessly gave a concert as a tribute to Whitney with the ladies Rombley and Grace. First names are not necessary, no one outside the lowlands know them. The women claim the loudest that Whitney is an example for them. Oh, yeah? Now we have to listen to you as a kind of requiem?

I let my thoughts die a natural death as I navigate on the Linge, like the heron and minnow. Outwit life. Life outsmarted you too.

32.

SUICIDAL FRUIT FLY

It is not well with the fruit flies and especially the male fruit fly. The male fruit fly has suffered from depression and seeks solace in a drink. Just like before when it was clearly a male's role, the female fruit fly is now becoming more assertive especially in reproduction that there is now uncertainty and helplessness. Say no more. The constant rejection by females makes her reach for the bottle.

"Male fruit flies that have an active sex life go en masse to drink." U.S. scientists said in writing in the Science journal.

Now I almost feel sorry for these males but unfortunately they have ruined themselves.

It's not really that everything I am experiencing right now is immediately dead but fruit flies are really dead! Anyway, I've never understood what they do on this earth. The only one who has something to eat is the wasp but I do not think I really like it when they immediately starve and die.

Fruit flies have died.

A few weeks ago, I finally gathered the courage and take the paint brush in my hand. I need to do some hard work to freshen up my house again. With good humor, sandpaper and ammonia, I carefully make the surfaces smooth and clean and then set them layer by layer in the paint. You'll be glad if you think it will sit low but then there are the depressive suicidal male fruit flies! You cannot see them throughout the day but then suddenly they go with their fat ass down in the wet paint. They stick straight down and are not strong enough again to come out. Suicide is successful and painless. I'm given to this tendency to migrate to a chosen moment in their life but not in my wet paint!

I removed it with my finger, you see. It does not work so I wait until the paint is dry. The place where the suicide has taken place remains visible.

There is nothing else then sanding, ammonia and paints. Then again, two fruit flies collapsed to their death into my wet paint and have had enough: death to the fruit flies!

33.

OVER MY DEAD BODY

There's a bench in the Wilhelmina in March. The sun starts to get warmer and the first crocuses stabbed their stiff cups from the grass as I sit at the ducks in the pond to watch the storm in my head. It revolves around the free death. A death to order a menu, such as: whether or not to get married, come out of the closet, a rental or owner-occupied and determining that life is full term.

It is time to weigh how long it is worth to live by. I feel increasingly held accountable and hear voices in my head: *"Hey ma, have you already made a statement? Do you want to be resuscitated? Now you have to choose if you plan to save Dad with a spoon in a plate and cry to your mother in the supermarket. That is preventable! You can get a dignified death at the needle of a doctor who has reconciled with his conscience and additional income like a pocket money. Say it! Determine your limits, if only for your peace of mind, Mom. Your life is not a do-it-yourself! We do not want to find a plastic bag over your head. You do not have the heart in your body to induce a "collision with a person". The NS is already a mess because you have nothing to contribute and you should not think that the supply of antidepressants and sleeping pills in your bedside table is enough to say goodbye, not even with a liter bottle of whiskey. The only thing that happened was that after a few days, you'll wake up in your urine. That will get you out of your mind, huh?"*

That goes through my head while I sit peacefully in the spring sunshine. In the distance is a young woman with an empty buggy. The child waddles in front with a bag of bread for the ducks. They have the time.

I'm on my heels by the thought which now stuck and must form an opinion as to when it will be when it is no longer worthy, too expensive or too much to handle, enough for posterity. I always assumed that I would sleep peacefully but that hardly seems to occur in reality. There are few people who do not get a push in the right direction. *"Give her no food because she balks when feeding, no drinking because she chokes and not antibiotics and antidepressants for the haunting in the night. Give her something to relax for the day, immediately because she is extremely recalcitrant, always have been."*

It is cold and dark in the park. I stand on the threshold of a new world. I am of age and I'm not prepared. It must not be said but I hang out with all my fiber of existence. I do not dread getting lost in the city, to be throwing food and cursing. The doctor takes out the poop in my nightgown. When I come to lie in the hospital, l I paste all the connectors by tightening *Leukoplast* and breathe until the bitter end.

34.

DIAMOND

Intense, sonorous, and with the velvety softness of dew. The pace, at first was soft and slow became quick and loud. I hear a symphony with allegro's adagio and allegretto's. Everything follows a natural logic if Bach had strung the chords themselves. This very pleasant sound is divine, like angels singing.

I have never heard an exhaust before tuned in color like a Stradivarius. The true connoisseur will immediately understand what I sing about in this eulogy: XT 500, the eighth wonder of the world. This is because even in appearance, this engineering feat had unprecedented greatness. Rarely did a designer style lines so perfect. The modern and traditional forms carry a pas de deux which leads to an ultimate climax of beauty in color and form, elegance and power. Robust power united with the agility of a deer is a huge experience when riding on this motorcycle. It rightly speaks of *'diamond'* in the crown of industrial design.

It's true that the traffic in the Netherlands is a shit, horrible, all provoking and I hate it! I just got back from holiday in an abandoned French province where I've seen a grand total of three lights in two weeks time and without danger, rode a hundred on a country road. I'm still among thousands of moronic motorists, none of whom can run without exception on a land where the greatest pleasure is achieved from walking forth in a wobbled pace from obstruction to obstruction. The country annually settled for kilometers of asphalt from my tax money, resulting in an inverse proportional distance to backup.

Each year, after the holidays, I fall into the same pit.

Every year, I like to dive into bed with a bottle of whiskey behind the curtains. Or buy via Marketplace, a Leopard tank, not once and not powerless, to participate in the movement portion. Maybe moving to a desert is even the best option.

Oh no, I hate sand in my socks, I'm a pacifist and I do not like whiskey.

The habituation process takes about a week. Then I'm back to the dull, as sheepish as everyone to participate in this clumsy highway game. Then I get the pleasure back from the passing of the traffic backup on my rumbling XT. I set myself up for the queue, waiting for the green light. Then I pull the throttle open and I see in my mirror the slow string disappearing at my back.

Well, there will be a traffic light again but here, I will be jealous as I gaze at passing cars where I will be first in line.

35.

WHAT A YEAR!

Yes, it's a holiday again, there you say to it: pooh, pooh! I am looking forward to it all year, the wonderful relaxation and rest because what vacation literally means is rest. How is it that your holiday is most stressful? In particular, it begins in advance when your wife wants to decorate the first period of the holiday which must be matched indoors because she's ready. You would rather go later in the holiday season because then, you have to look forward to everything. Your daughter wants to in the weeks that her friends are on holiday. *Pffff.* Then you are at home to agree and then go to work. There you try to vote on who goes where with your colleagues. That one colleague always bail out on sooner than you and you're back with yourself and could not properly assert your choice so you get home and have to choose that for you again. You always feel the dick and it seems that no one takes you into account. You pull home with the blame because you know from experience that a discussion is pointless. You act like you want to pass through with their choice well. They are beautiful enough not to give you the blame. This year, you want to do something different. It is embarrassing to go to the same camp in Drenthe as you've done in years because you cannot come up with anything else.

You all sit at the table together behind the computer. Your daughter will find nothing like she was 13. There is no disco. I do not think the pool is beautiful. That is for the elderly. That's too far from the shops. Eventually they looked at Turkey and booked everything via internet. Go now, pay next year; all inclusive. Ideal especially when you speak of paying next year because saving does not really work. There are still a number of payment plans. The TV broke and so you get a new one but immediately bought a flat of course. The kitchen needs to be replaced in accordance with your wife and you were whining sick about her. A new kitchen to use has to have all the desired appliances for your wife the previous year. Well let it be black with a pair of Poland and still save a lot of money. Then there was smoke from the machine and you cannot do without a laptop and your daughter who had not yet been paid off and a truly American Bully should have vaccine. Actually, there was no money for the holidays this year but yes, you were right there too.

36.

ʀENATE

She knew it was dangerous, perhaps fatal yet Renate put the bag down in the middle of the dining room. Of course it was not the bag that was dangerous but what's in it.

Pip, her cat jumped on the table and sniffed the bag. It was disappointed because it was not a fish or anything else edible so it slunk off again.

Renate sat on the couch and lit a cigarette. She just wanted a quiet time before she would open the bag.

She was walking past the shop this morning ten times before she dared to go inside. When she had put herself, she finally admitted she felt her heart pounding in her throat. Her breathing quickened and she noticed that she blushed. She glanced around to see if there were no acquaintances in the store. How embarrassing it would be if she would come against one of her friends from here. Luckily, it was quiet in the city and most people were just working. Renate had specially made quite a day here.

The front of the store had toys, in all colors and sizes. The back had layers of DVDs which was sorted by topic. An older man was standing with two DVDs in his hands. On the cover of one were two black men and at the other was something about dwarves. Looks like the man doubted that he would take the DVD.

Renate himself knew exactly what she wanted. She walked off on one of the shelves she targeted. She picked up a pink and white box and walked quickly to the checkout. A bored-looking man just looked at the right price and asked if she wanted it in a bag.

Renate softly said no, she had taken a Blokker bag herself.

In the tram home, she constantly had the feeling that everyone could see what was in her bag. To be safe, she clutched the Blokker bag even closer to her. She was sure it was opaque; she had tried it at home.

Now she was home and got the bag on the table. Renate got up and took the box out from the bag.

Two weeks later, the police rammed the door of Renate's apartment open. The neighbors had complained about the smell and the letters were visibly piled high behind her door. Two officers found Renate lifeless in her bedroom. When they saw the open box on the dining room table, they looked at each other.

"*Tarzan!*" one said. The other nodded: "*People should know better.*"

Tarzan had created a victim again.

37.

TELEVISION

The television set was still not in every home in the sixties. Children knew who possessed a TV and would go near. The trick was to get a place in the tube on the Wednesday and Saturday afternoon show. You would be sitting together in a darkened room with ten other children with feet in stockings and hands washed with the coconut matting. Cheers and applause rose up when the presenter called Aunt Hannie, the gray-white snow image of a 30 by 30 appeared. You've got to have pretty good eyes and a vivid imagination to be able to follow a program but that was of secondary importance.

My neighbors, an old couple in their 70s owned a television. The neighbor was fond of me so my place was assured. However, there was a downside. The neighbor was a lung patient and it seemed that the *telly* had a tingling effect on her windpipe. There was not much to see from the picture because of poor reception and there were also large parts of the text taken off by the constant coughing.

Luckily, my neighbor was deaf. He would watch with us with the volume knob so high that the speakers blared. The condition of the neighbor was perceived less positively by my parents. The daily TV broadcast could be followed word for word in our house through the wall without protest. Did people used to be more tolerant?

What annoyed me as well with my neighbor were her feet. If I could find no other place, I sat cross-legged on her chair. The neighbor had to kick the habit of removing her shoes off. Then, she rubbed the hideous knobby feet in flesh-colored stockings, striking them against each other. The calluses gave a grinding sound that gave me goose bumps. Moreover, this resulted to dust clouds. I held my shirt over my nose because I was afraid to breathe the sour smelling stuff.

You could be waiting halfway through the program when the neighbor presents a slice of *Arretje* cake, a mixture of cocoa butter and crumbled Maria biscuits. I always refused with an excuse.

This afternoon, they had made the cake stand in the kitchen. I heard the coughing through the thin wall. In my mind I saw phlegm and alveoli mingle with the ingredients of the cake.

No, in all respects, it was a blessing when we got ourselves a television a few years later.

s V

38.
CIVILIZATION?

Civilization Van Dale: the state of mental and moral development.

Young boys, still children, were abused by representatives of the Catholic Church with some even years on end by several priests. Bishops have known it but the case is only dealt internally. Even parents who were blind to the signs of their children and the subject took off with "*Oh, it'll be easy.*" The spiritual leader of this movement calls himself the vicar of God on earth! They will do something only after charges were proven against a large number of his priests which is a weak excuse. He promises improvement but not penance.

They are still abusing the pariahs of society in the home of the Pope, the pious Italy. They still would not face it. The Pope states in several Western European countries and America about an inquiry but does so only under the pressure of public opinion.

How is it possible that an organization where its representatives imposes celibacy, condemns homosexuality and condom use, bans abortion and abuses children has the guts to say that God is love? Is it the pulpit civilization?

Young boys and even girls who are abused by governments as child soldiers are set to battle against what? Governments put children in the front lines. Burundi, Sudan and even the United States are some examples. Other countries like Colombia, Uganda and Zimbabwe are supporting paramilitary groups that use child soldiers. Governments promise to adhere to the UN Convention to stop child soldiers. Research by Amnesty International shows that at least 60 governments including Netherlands and Germany have not yet ratified the treaty and 16 and 17-year olds are recruits. This is so in order to hide them by giving them status as *"aspiring soldier "*. Is this civilization?

Young boys and girls, even children, are exploited for labor. Child labor rate is at 180 million children worldwide, mostly caused by poverty. They are sold by their parents as laborers or end up in prostitution. They lack education and future prospects. Governments and churches are not able to make an end to this civilization.

Civilization does not exist; not in public and not even in churches.

Civilization is made by the individual. That one brother or sister could be anywhere in the world like a small hospital or school found by those passionate individuals who offer a new perspective for fifteen years in Sierra Leone as child soldiers. The funds for their work are often acquired through their own efforts or any organization consisting mainly of volunteers: War Child, Amnesty International and Defense for Children. For them, that's the real civilization.

39.

TRACK POINT

Mix 100g of breadcrumbs, 100g cake crumbs, 3 tablespoons of honey and mix it well. Put the mixture into a round cake pan and press it well and set it on a pan of water. There are points of intersection. Behold…the track points: a typical Utrecht recipe that originated in the crisis years.

Utrecht. I have nothing although recently I was in town and had an hour to spare. I decided to make it past the places that make me walk through Utrecht. *Nieuwegracht* is where I went to school. Once my father found that primary school in our (farmers) village was not good enough to prepare me for the future. Therefore, as a ten year old boy, I cycled back and forth daily to the big city to finish the last three years of my primary school and then at the same school, *"The Gregory"* will follow for further education. Even on Sunday, I'd cycle there voluntarily to sing in prison with the boys on the Wolvenplein.

Further, on the same canal later, I started my first job at the Catholic newspaper *"The Centre"*. I fell in love with Anneke, the long, dark girl dressed in flower power. There's Elizabeth, the daughter of a farmer's cheese maker from Woerden. There's also Willy, an unattainable beauty in hot pants. She was already with someone and then, Jeanine. Ah, Jeanine! I did break walks with her and we were always at our bakery in Nobelstraat to make a dime at picking track points and we were addicted to it.

I found Lombok in the Utrecht neighborhood where I first lived independently. Besides Utrecht, I lived as a 'guest worker' for Spaniards, Italians and Turks. Immigrant was only a word from the dictionary. My neighbor in the upper house next door was a Turk. He lived there with six compatriots. No one wondered who they were, what they did and whether they should be here. They did, after all the jobs that we ourselves do not want to do.

In summer, Ali went to Turkey for six weeks. First, he came to the coffee shop and told me that I do not have to worry about his countrymen for he had quite drummed for their cause. No noise or nuisance; never heard of them.

After returning home, Ali thanked me for the match at his house with a typical Turkish delicacy: Halva I gave him a *'welcome home'* with…track points.

40.

UTREG

Every time I go through downtown on my bike, I taste the beauty of it. When was the first time that her gracefulness stroked my eyes? The canals that meander through the greenery lined with facades of city palaces which in my eyes is the most beautiful on earth. There's Old Dutch pomp in the museum for a quarter with its courtyards, parks, arches and turrets. The rugged town hall with its baroque appearance can even compete with the Palace on Dam Square. A little further from the heart is the patrician luxury with poetic names under the eaves. They are just as enchanting as the tiny arm houses a little further. The sunlight plays in the stained-glass windows.

What about the churches? In no other city did I see such beauty as clerically concentrated here. Places of worship of any size but with the same charm. The cathedral was built by megalomaniacs. Cathedral: a standard for many towers and churches elsewhere in the country. So was our creator to be honored. This city is compact and well-organized, around and off like a Swarovski egg, not vulgar and exaggerated.

Still, I need little something from the heart but noted futility during cycling.

The crowds, the tourists!

They are miserable wretches with cameras that chatters take my city in possession. In wide rows, only extreme vigilance can prevent a collision. Suicidal lemmings will collapse the unwary under your front wheel.

Besides, what's really annoying is this: the 35,000 students who pollute my city. They do not take it so closely with decency. There are brief, rolling barrels and bleating drunkards who live in the city as a big orgy.

Talk about partying. The young people from the suburbs can also be rarely seen and heard with so much aggression as flat at night in the center. I wonder if it's the "Utrègs ÛN dialectical or UN *sproakgebrek (I don't understand this word)*.

A corrective note of an older person is no longer appreciated. Many times I have to make my feet off to avoid bodily injury. It's not just threats; a witness gets molested in the bus shelters and cars in their wake.

Cycling incidentally, is wonderful in our city but the bike store is asking for trouble. Just go into a store to do an errand and you risk a bent front wheel. Or worse, if your bike is stolen for the umpteenth time, you'll have bad luck because driving is made impossible by the city council. The introduction of an incomprehensible way makes your system crazy. Is your vehicle losing the insufficient parking chance? There are also traffic jams caused by permanently broken roads.

If you manage to store your car and you want to celebrate a lager, then there is the annoyance of the crowded terrace. Grab your seat if you're lucky, you should only see that you can order what you can consume. The staff (recruited *studentenvee—I don't understand this*) is in fact only concerned with themselves able to chat in their smartphone.

In short, there is a metropolitan annoyance in a provincial town.

Litter and dog dirt, beggars, dealers, pickpockets...

Yet…give me *Utreg (I don't understand this)*!

41.

LANDLADY

It was sometime in October and I cycled from a party in the city of Utrecht to my room. I had quite a few drinks but my sense of direction was not affected by the alcohol…or so I thought. Of course it did not help that it's 5:15 in the morning and that there was not a soul on the street you could ask.

Anyway, it was not necessary since I certainly knew where I was going. It was a pity that I had no idea where I am at that moment.

A month earlier, I had almost all districts of Utrecht seen in my mind when I was looking for an affordable, clean, cozy, not too far from the center but still quiet but if necessary, preferably from rooftop air balcony room in a dorm. That this student dorm was populated by incredibly handsome but smart blondes was obvious.

Unfortunately, I found only a woman of 70 in the gray garret of Tuindorp hotel district. I have nothing against a neighborhood where most residents have lived through the war (for clarity: the Second World War, not the Gulf War), but usually these are not the neighborhoods where it is still buzzing after dinner and sparkles.

I had to settle for this little room out of necessity after I had seen that most student houses had incredibly handsome but smart blondes especially looking for new housemates who are also incredibly handsome, intelligent and painfully blonde.

From my landlady allowed me my room from Monday morning to Friday afternoon. She probably thought she could enjoy because I do not come half drunk every Friday or Saturday night after stepping down the stairs and stumbling upon her on a calm weekend. What she did not know was that the students living in Utrecht had its climax experience on Thursday; that after stepping half drunk up the stairs stumbled every Thursday night as a result, after I had first puked properly across the gnomes in her garden.

I cycled Thursday night and Friday morning to my room but had no idea where I was. At one point I saw a truck standing with beside Stellaard bakery. After the driver that the fix was asked where I could find the Zwaardemaker Avenue, he said that I (and I quote) articulately clear as possible: "It's really very, very far away…" Either that or I just had too much.

It was cold, the sun came up, my head hurt, I was sick and I was on the wrong side of town.

When I was cycling over an hour later to my district, with an unrecognized street, I had vomited on the garden gnome and found out that I had lost my key so I rang the bell. There was some stumbling, some keys rattled in the locks, some cut were pushed aside and there stood Mrs. Landlady in a bathrobe and with bad hair. I wiped my mouth, hugged her and started kissing while tears of joy ran down my face against her exuberant hair.

The joy was unfortunately short-lived. I had to find a new room again the next day…preferably with a roof, of course.

SV

42.

OH, WOE, OH SMART

September: December starts.

The first gingerbread cookies are on the shelves. A child whines.

"No, it is still far from Santa Claus!"

Dear child does not give up: *"Mom, I'm still **waiting!**"*

"No! Stop it!"

The boy angrily runs away from her. Then he sees me. I encourage him and point to the gingerbread bags and make a gesture of *'good'*. He put on a scream.

"Shut up, bitch," his mother hisses at him.

She sees that I heard it but she perseveres. At the checkout, she discovered a bag of ginger nuts in her basket. Destructive, she looks at her child but she keeps it and paid. I quickly leave the store with a nod to the boy.

October: it smells of December.

At the entrance to the garden center is a donut stall. The most horrifying singing reindeers and Santa Clauses lure you into the Christmas circus. I want no Christmas! I want a bag of gravel for the garden. On the way to the checkout, I encountered a typical proposal.

*"We will set up a bridge in the garden with such **Christmas goblin**? That one!"*

I'm going to drink coffee. There too was a couple.

They sit next to me! Within 15 minutes, I knew all about them: the man had 30 years in the construction industry. *"Worn back sir."*

About the woman: *"**Fibro…fibroma** …well, you know, sir."*

On their huge flat screen: *"Full HD, sir."*

They have participated in the election of the most beautifully decorated Christmas street in the Netherlands.

"We have a good chance, sir."

They pay for my coffee and go again.

I meet the couple again at the box office and see the amount on the display at € 835.65!

November: December is gaining momentum.

Sinterklaas arrives. Shopping in the city today is not a party. The center is populated by countless mothers and fathers with ornate estate tricycles containing their buck kiddies. The Mayor announces the arrival of the deadly serious and good Saint.

December: let it snow, let it snow…Sinterklaas presents.

Christmas dinner, fireworks and music; cover Queen *Trijntje* surrenders her Christmas CD over to a late 19th century tunes; even worse is The Summit 2000 with the top off the rock group Queen, for the umpteenth time their Bohemian Rhapsody.

I wish I were stranded on a ferry to Schiermonnikoog.

Plus Dot: the daughter-to-be and their son had proposed to jointly organize a Christmas dinner.

Have yourself a merry little Christmas.

43.

NOT SO SMART

I have a new mobile phone, such a smartphone with a touch screen. I am very happy with it. I can see three weeks ahead what the weather will be in Sliedrecht: cloudy here and there with a drop of rain. The average temperature is 12 degrees during the day. I'm not sure, but it seems pretty cool for the time of year and certainly for Sliedrecht. Besides, I am not in Sliedrecht for three weeks but it's amazing what my phone can do. Example, I can accurately determine where I am up to two meters. The GPS does it so I stood in the middle of the last in Neude in Utrecht and I thought, let's see if my phone can see where I am now!

I clicked on Google Earth, there was a world scoop around and it twisted: my phone, I was standing in the middle of the Neude in Utrecht; clever, huh?

Furthermore, there is speech recognition. I mispronounced the names of my friends and as it is, I get a surprise every time with whomever I get on the line.

For example, if I say, *"Call Astrid!"* then my smartphone will be calling one Rachid whom I do not know. I do not know how my phone comes to Rachid's number but it seems he's not a nice man. After I tried last night to call Astrid 17 times, he shouted through the phone with things about my mother. Moreover, I have no idea how Rachid knew my mother.

What is also very special about this is I can scan groceries in the store with my phone. When I'm in the C1000, a net of oranges from €3, 49 suits and barcode scanning, then I hear a bleep and there on my screen comes: *"Just oranges, €3, 49."* I love it. Last week, I've also been through C1000 to scan anything. A pack of *Chocolate Dreams Verkade* showed on my phone, a suit of Edet Wet toilet paper should be there. I am the branch manager there so at the takeoff, he should also have scanned the *Chocolate Dreams* with his own scanner but he just stood there as *Chocolate Dreams* came on the screen. I do not quite trust it so I went to the supermarket on the other side of the neighborhood. I've not encountered misleading barcodes so far.

Actually, I do not speak to so many friends since I got my new phone.

How would it be with Rachid?

44.

H●RNY

The 60s and 70s: years of Love, Peace and Flower power through Sex, Drugs and Rock & Roll. They were also the years of student protests, riots and squatters emancipation. It was in short, the years of opposition to the established order.

Sexual freedom has become sexual consumption. Use of drugs has evolved from a good-natured trip to addiction. Squatter riots are reduced to a few dozen protesters in the left-most city in the Netherlands (!). The wave of emancipation was a weak sequel in the 70s but got no further than a handful of women at the top. Women continue to populate the schoolyards and detergent commercials are mostly still touted by women.

With the theme *"Women at Work"*, the original German farmer nail Hornbach in a brochure wants us to believe that women are tough handymen. They do this by showing up in tight W@WT-dressed women on jerseys for display like breaking in brick, drilling and wallpapers with income vamps. To put their claim to power, they illustrate the brochure with evocative images and texts. In addition to the illustration of a crooked nail beaten with a few drops of blood and beside it is the text: *"My first time with Hornbach."*

On top of a supine woman lie a number of robust and ergonomic tools that are extremely smooth and good in the hand."

The text here is: *"Do it yourself"*.

Elsewhere the remark was: *"Size does matter"*.

The advertising agency that devised the campaign calls this *"an ode to the female job"*. Sic!

Girls, women, mothers and daughters take it! Go up to the nearest Hornbach: demolition walls and nail doors. Paint the house pink and show that you cannot only have renovation with your chest but also your bathroom.

Whether you secretly see the humor or not in Hornbach, you'll find it in your heart to be pleasing that the neighbor's sink was unstoppable, your husband is in the papers room and a passer (obviously a man) can swap your tire or simply put in other words: *"Women still hear in the kitchen!"*

CPSIA information can be obtained at www.ICGtesting.com
Printed in the USA
BVOW05s1516230415

397463BV00001B/23/P